Two Little Chicks

by Valeri Gorbachev

NorthSouth
New York / London

One fine day, Mother Hen took her two little chicks to the playground for the very first time.

Such a busy playground!
The little chicks felt scared.

They saw two dogs on the seesaw.

"Hop on!" called the dogs.

"Oh, no!" said the chicks.

"Little chicks can't do THAT!"

They saw three pigs on the
merry-go-round.

"Want a ride?" called the pigs.

"Oh, no!" said the chicks.

"Little chicks can't do THAT!"

They saw two big cats on
the swings.

"Want to swing?" called
the cats.

"Oh, no!" said the chicks.
"Little chicks can't do THAT!"

They saw four frogs and
four mice playing on the slide.
Up, up, up they climbed, then
wheeee! down they slid.

"Climb on up," said a mouse.
"You're next."

"Oh, no!" said the chicks.
"Little chicks can't do THAT!"

"We're little too," said
the mouse. "You can do it."

"Well," said one chick.

"Maybe . . ." said the
other chick.

And step by step, they
climbed up the ladder.

But when they got to the
top, the little chicks were afraid.
"Slide down!" shouted a frog.
"We can't!" cried the little
chicks.

"Everybody is afraid the first time," said Beaver. "Let's slide down together. Just climb on my tail and hold tight."

The little chicks held on tight
and closed their eyes.

"*Whee!*" said Beaver, and
down the slide they went.

"*Whee! Whee!*" cried the little
chicks as they got to the bottom.
"Let's do it again."

And they climbed right back
up the ladder.

"Look!" they shouted.
"We're going to slide down all
by ourselves!"

And that's just what they did.

"Hooray!" everyone cheered.
"Let's play all day!"
"Little chicks CAN do
THAT!" cried the chicks.